**PRESS FIVE PUBLISHING(2020)**

PRESS FIVE PUBLISHING
2020 SECRETS

Aaron Morris @officialpressfive
Amazon: Family Ties, Trust is Rare, Secrets. @pressfive_books

**2020 SECRETS**

**"WE NEVER WANTED MUCH, JUST A LITTLE RESPECT"**

**-The Author**

**SECRETS**

2020 PRESS FIVE PUBLISHING

## Paying The Bills.....

The tear's rolling down Richie's face made clear lines through the blood that covered him, the gag in his mouth muffled his cry's as he sat there.
It had been hours since Bobby and Nicky had caught him slipping out the back door to his mother's house, noon into the early night Richie was beaten like it was a hobby.

Bobby nor Nicky had any emotion for the half dead man sitting in front of them, this was business and they only came for the check.

"Holy Shit Richie, who the fuck did this to you,"? Joey asked, laughing as he came strolling into the basement from the steps.

Richie's eyes barely able to open, as he cried out muffled screams to Joey.

Joey looked around the basement, it was covered in wall to wall plastic – even the floors.

Richie's beaten body sat dead center of the room, Bobby and Nicky stood there hungry for a order to end him from Joey.

"Cut it off," Joey said, unbuttoning his blazer and sliding his thick arms from the jacket in one Smooth motion.

"His head or his hands Boss,"? Bobby asked, stepping in closer with Nicky close on his side.

"The gag Bobby," Joey replied shaking his head.

Bobby grabbed Richie by his hair and jerked his head as he slide a blade under the cotton gag stuffed in his mouth.
Richie took in the biggest gasp of air his lungs could take as the gag fell free from his mouth.

Joey's House.....

Joey was up early, his nerves wouldn't allow his body to stay still and his thoughts kept his mind racing like a dope head looking to score.
A loud noise sounded off in the other room from where he stood in the kitchen, he reached over towards a black box hanging above the light switch and a loud click snapped then the room was silent again.

"Top of the money, the mafuckin money," Nicky said, stepping into the kitchen with a smile from ear to ear.
"And the money will always be on top," Joey replied along with him, swinging a hand out to his friend.

"How you feeling Boss,"? Nicky asked, pulling out a chair at the island wrapping around the large kitchen.

"Normally I would be nervous before a job Nick, but I woke up feeling different today,"

"Yeah I haven't slept since you said it was a go – Nicky paused – I mean we pulled jobs but nothing on our own,"

Joey looked over at his best friend since preschool, "Well shit just changed,"

(5:00am Eastside Wilmington Delaware)

Nicky had gotten to the wear house two hours ahead of the rest, Joey was making sure everything was set in stone and things would fall on time. This wasn't a risk anyone was willing to take for the fuck of it, this had to mean every second of it.

Joey pulled the heavy dump truck up as close as possible, Tony sat parked directly in front of him. He noticed everyone was waiting and ready, he had to keep the smile from growing ace his lips as he dipped into the wear house doors.

Joey thought to himself as he came into view with everyone there waiting on him – Today was already beginning to feel great.

Good morning Boss," Tony Greeted Joey as he walked in.

"Good morningggggg Bossssss," came a few different voices behind laughter.

"Nicky enough with the bullshit, were family but there remains a level of respect among men. He's one of us, no one lives among us in disrespect. So treat him with the same respect you have for yourself, were all men here." Joey cut in, taking the moment of laughter right from under them all.

"Just yanking his balls Boss," Nicky answered.

Joey shook his head and handed the room over to Val, he was running the show from a far – and this was as far as he was going.

"Everybody here understands the route,"? Valentino asked, looking around the room. "Nicky and Willie truck one, Tony and me truck two. Andy will seal the deal at the light, and remember the exit fellas,"

Joey gave Val a head nod and called to Nicky.

(5:00am Riverside Housing,  Wilmington Delaware)

Wilmington's FBI and ATF were having a ruff morning,  it wasn't even 5 in the morning and the whole department was up and under crime scene lights.

Agent were called after the trash company came across blood running from a small black trash can, non of the workers touched a thing. Old guy driving said he seen things like this before, after all he said he had 20 years on the job and felt it in his gut to just call the cops.

"Somebody thinks it's trash day huh,"? Agent Jackson said, stepping onto the sidewalk.

"Yeah – Agent Allen replied pausing for a second – they left him outside his mother's house, you think it's a message,"? He asked, looking over to Agent Jackson.

"The message is clear, somebody fucked up, question now is who was the message left for,"? He asked, not to Agent Allen directly but in general.

"Holy fucking Christ,"

Agent Jackson stepped around to get the same view as Allen had just gotten.  – FUCK -
was all he could say as he took in the same scene as his fellow officer.

The deceased was cut into the smallest piece either officer had ever seen, the bag looked like a raw package off meat.

Jackson looked over at Allen, "Do we have a positive ID on the vic,"? He asked, still looking back to the trash bag.

“Mother said it’s her son, they left his hand on her door step. She identified him by the ring left on his finger,” Allen replied, looking away towards where the mother stood with the rest of the family.

Joey left as the boys got their shit together, he had a alibi to make and being with them wasn’t it.

“Let’s roll,” Nicky barked, as he jumped in the passenger seat of the dump truck.

Joey set the job up for 5 guys, Nicky and Val had been with Joey since preschool, Andy, Tony, and Willie came along years later. But the bond between the gang was unbreakable, secrets among the 5 were stories only to be told to the devil himself.

Two stolen dump trucks and a off the grid ambulance, the crew was planned for the best and the worst at this time. The only thoughts raving inside each man’s mind was the sounds of a Money  Machine ringing, that and sex on white sand in the islands of St.Thomas.

Most of the ride Nicky was silent, his eyes told Tony most of what he wanted to ask but thought it be best to remain quiet. First time any of them went out on their own, let alone a job under the table.

Andy beamed in over the two way radio, "Take up parking and get comfortable, next move is our best move stay ready fellas,"

Tony looked both ways from the passenger side, if this worked out he prayed the family never found out.

Andy came beaming back again over the two way, "hey fellas watch for any unmarked the city is crawling with fucking feds, we gotta stay ten steps ahead of these hard dick pricks."

"Stop fucking thinking so bad luck you idiot, no time for that shit stay in the fucking game," Nicky shot back over the radio.

Val looked over at Willie and shook his head, "Nicky is a ball breaker ain't he,"

Willie shook his head and Let out a  small laugh under his breath. "Yeah he's a fucking nut cracker,"

Nicky flipped open a cheap phone and pushed a small chip in the side and powered the phone up, he pressed a few buttons and waited till a voice came on the other end. Nicky closed the phone shut and passed it over to Tony, he instantly opened the phone and snapped it in half.

Val came calling over the speaker, "alright ladies don't let your panties smother your balls, let them hang, we can't afford to lose anything,"

Each man moved their lips silently, there was a old saying – Never step foot in the fire without speaking to the devil, unless you were there to take the house."

Agent Jackson was on a call when Agent Allen walked over and tapped him on the shoulder, “Boss you might want to hear what the mother has to say.” Allen informed him looking a little shaken up.

Jackson looked over to where he had last seen the victims mother then said a few words into his cell phone and hung up.

“But we gotta take this somewhere else,” Allen said stopping Jackson before he got to the side walk.

Jackson looked up and back over at Allen, “ take her to the safe house,”

Allen didn’t reply, he took a step and waved his hand for Ms. Winchester.

“Excuse me Ms. Winchester this is Agent Kevin Jackson. Would you mind following us mama,”? Agent Allen asked, looking around for any eyes that may be on them and them alone.

The older lady stepped off the curb with the help of Agent Allen, she held onto his arm the whole way to the car without speaking a word.

(7:25am Bank of America)

Smithfield held the back door of the bank open for his Coworker, the sun was beginning to shine and the temperature was starting to warm up.

"We're taking 11th down and over the bridge, no more stops on this route call base and tell them we're headed back." Clayton said, rolling the two large bags out to the truck.

"What happen to the other pick ups,"? Smithfield asked, slamming the bank door behind him and calling over the radio to their coworkers waiting inside the armored truck. "26 and 27 at the back,"

The radio clicked back but was unclear to hear.

Once inside Clayton locked the bags and seat back in his seat. The bank gave us two million dollars, the company doesn't allow use to transport anything above that so we gotta head back, then pick up our route," Clayton explained, clicking off of the two way headset that all 4 men were carrying.

"Long day fellas," Johnson replied back.

"More money more problems," Clayton said laughing at the face Smithfield had.

"Guess a little over time ain't do bad right," Smithfield shot back to the men.

“Yeah now you can get your lady that ring she wants,” Johnson yelled back over his shoulder from the front of the truck.

“You ok up there Clarkson,”? Clayton asked, smacking his hard against the metal penal between him and the front of the armor truck where Clarkson sat.

“Yes sir what about yourself,”? He asked back, looking straight out the window as they drove on.

Andy was so focused his neck was starting to hurt, he looked straight, then to his left, then to his right, he was keeping his eyes peeled.

Before he could turn to look right once more he seen the truck turn down 11th street, he jerked up in his seat and grabbed the two way radio.

“Get ready boys, we got company coming up?” Andy whispered, pushing the timer on his dashboard.

Nicky kept the truck in drive the whole time, keeping his foot pressed against the break. The truck turned onto 11$^{th}$ and Tony and Nicky were right behind them, the morning work traffic was a beautiful sight.

"Keep it close we don't want to make a gap, don't need any guest." Tony said, gripping the door handle.

Nicky looked over for a split second before slamming his eyes back on the truck ahead, he was going to keep it safe but no space.

"Tony get Val on the line tell him when that truck swings right they better have the ass light as a welcome sign for these cocksuckers," Nicky barked, keeping his head straight and his hands glued to the wheel

Tony didn't hesitate, he gripped the two way and started yelling for Val, before Val could finish completely Andy's lights lit up and the plan was set. The truck's right blinker popped on and Val let the break go from his foot and swung the heavy dumpster out onto the street and slammed it in break.

Nicky hit the right turn without letting up from the gas, a wicked smile spread across his face the second he seen Val and Willie blocking the rest of Clifford Brown off from traffic as Nicky blocked the armored truck in from the back.

It was like a scene out of the movie with Ben Affleck - The Town – Val and Willie came Ambushing towards the armor truck, Nicky and Tony were hot coming up the back.

Johnson nor Clarkson could have seen it coming, but the red tank's caught their attention but it was caught a little to late.

Johnson reached for the panic button but couldn't see, the truck was filling up with thick smoke from the safety holes on the doors. The holes were might to fire through if a robbery was to take place, which was now but Johnson and Clarkson were under attack and to them it was in the dark.

Smithfield ducked low as soon as the first blast came through the back, he was a little ahead of the smoke so he had his hands already on his firearm at the pull.

The four tossed the fire extinguishers, got into action immediately dropping in concussion grenades then taking cover at the front and back of the truck.

The blast sent the truck shaking, Nicky was up on his feet and Tony was on his hip making every move with him. Both men peeled back this thick like tape from two Frags, and placed them on both of the doors locks.

It was Joey's idea to go with the Frags, they were H.E (High Explosive) and got the job done in one shot.

There are several types of grenades like the Frags, high explosive (HE) concussion and Smoke grenades, the used Frags and fire extinguishers.
Fragmentation grenades are probably the most common in modern armies. They are missiles designed to disperse shrapnel on detonation.

The back doors went flying the second the explosives blasted off, the ringing was a head bleed in itself but the team was ready for it.

Val swing around to the driver door and sent two shots into the windshield, the bullet just bounced off the armor truck. It was a scare tactic, as the team went for the back of the truck guns blazing like Pistol Pete.

Nicky seen the metal before the flame but still couldn't duck the fire, Smithfield let his finger off the trigger he still couldn't see the powder from the extinguishers was caked in his eyes. Tony didn't miss a beat he started firing back inside the truck.

"Let's go let's go," someone was screaming into the headset.

The four of them could see everything the gas mask were keeping them in the clear, they wasted no time jumping inside the back and started tossing out bags.

Willie noticed one of the armor truck employees in the front was trying wipe the window, he dropped down and set off shots at the passenger door just as it cracked open.

Willie knew he missed as the passenger slide down and ducked behind the parked car on its right.

"Got one on the loose fellas," Willie barked into the headset, almost dropping yo his knees as he slide along the parked cars.

Clarkson mumbled something to himself and jumped up from behind a car, Willie was one car up from him in the opposite direction. It took less then a second for Willie to spin on his heels, Clarkson's head snapped forward like he was ducking.

The shot cracked his skull open, brain matter from the back was in his throat. His face hit the ground before he was fully off of his feet, his body fell to the concrete like a bag of sand.

Johnson came flying out the passenger side, he took off running like Usain Bolt, his feet seem to not even touch the ground. If running for your life was a person he was the poster boy for it, but his run was cut down fast as he ran right into Valentino coming to check on Willie.

Shell after shell bounced off the blacktop, Val's finger was burning from squeezing the trigger like a mad man. His blood was on boil and his hands were inching for money, today wasn't the day to play super hero he thought to himself.

"Let's rollllllll," nobody could see Nicky but they all knew it was his voice coming in over the headset.

Val got closer to Johnson, he was basically standing over top of him when he lifted his gun and sent two bullets crashing into his face.

Every men bent the next corner like they were running for the fence in a jail break movie, Andy was waiting with the ambulance lights flashing.

The only thing in sight was darkness, each man had their eyes closed saying something that could have been taken as a prayer.

The 911 call that came over the radio sounded more like the day the World Trade Centers fell to the street's of New York. The panic in the first response team calls back for all available units was chilling, the scene was being described like a mess shooting.

Agent Jackson and Allen were only a block away when the call came in about the bank truck robbery, anything related to the treasury department was a federal offense.

Allen was calling into the office for their boss as they pulled onto Clifford Brown, trying to make their way as far down as they could by car. The block was a decent length, but the many lights and uniforms made the street look very close in size – it was a full party of Blue Bloods.

The top hats of the Bureau were all on the scene and from the looks – they had their cocks all tied in a knot and Allen was the first to notice the bullshit coming down.

"Jackson , Allen , where you parked,"? Donny DelMarco yelled from the group of big wigs.

"Corner of the block, why what's up Donny,"? Allen replied with a question of his own.

DelMarco spoke a few words towards the group and stepped off meeting Jackson and Allen at the back of the armor truck.

Dutch stood up from the hard bed he called a resting nest for the last 17 years, and looked himself over once more in his small mirror.

“Looking good Boss,” Tommy mumbled as he stood in the doorway to Dutch’s cell.

“The wife is here today,” Dutch replied, grabbing his federal inmate ID card off of his dresser before nodding to Tommy as he pushed through the door.

Dutch followed the lines through the Corridor headed to the visiting room, his heart was smelling but his face was mug. He was approaching 18 years soon stuck Inside these nasty penitentiary walls, there was nothing to smile about from the inside only the joy that came from those on the outside.

Marcy was standing there wide smile as Dutch came strolling into the visiting room, she had waited all month for their few hour visit. Since Dutch was shipped out to Inez Kentucky from another pen in West Virginia she only gotten a chance to fly once a month at His request, she never questioned his business so it was a Ordinary way of life for them now.

Dutch kissed her lightly on the lips before taking his seat, the prison was strict about Physical interaction between visitors and inmates and Dutch Avoided or problems if Possible.

“How was your flight Marcy,”? Dutch asked, looking his beautiful wife in her soft green eyes.

“Same as always, I have a few messages from Louie,” She replied opening a bag of the chips she had gotten him from one of the many snack Machines the prison offered the inmates and families.

DelMarco was straight to the punch when he approached the two.

“Fellas, this one is nasty and it’s all yours,”

Jackson looked past DelMarco towards the crowd then back over to his partner, “And you mean this is which ways Denny,”? Jackson asked, now looking him dead in the face.

“Mayor wants this in the organized crime unit,” Denny replied with a shrug of the shoulders.

Allen looked inside the truck from where he stood, “What do we have so far, when was this called in,”? He asked quickly, pulling a pair of gloves from his back pocket.

“Medical examiners are still going at it, but we have a positive ID on all of our victims, Truck just left Bank of America up on French street, load was carrying $2 Million dollars,” DelMarco informed the two on the scene before them.

“Here we have, Sean Smithfield and Chris Clayton, both multiple GSW’s and you can see from the ground the many different shell casings, this was no side job,” DelMarco said, looking back down to the note pad in his hands.

Jackson took a step towards the passenger side and started to walk along as DelMarco explained the scene as they knew it so far and Allen was close by taking pictures with his phone.

“It looks as if Clarkson, was trying to hold them off – DelMarco said pausing, taping the outline where a gun laid next to a police cone.
“Then we have him – DelMarco pointed towards the ground— That’s the driver, name is James Johnson, looks like he was going to make a run for it but they did him over, half the kids face is laying in the street,” DelMarco looked back towards the yellow tape blocking off the end block, “And I can bet my life no one seen or heard a thing,”

DelMarco walked the agents through the Entire Crime scene before taking off back to the office for some Research, the night was so far away and still they already had their hands full of work.

“Where do you want to start,”? Allen asked his partner.

“Let’s start with a phone call,” Jackson replied, pulling out his phone and walking towards the end block they had parked on.

Allen didn’t say a word as the two headed up the block, it wasn’t even the true break of dawn and the city on in a uproar.

Joey was pumped up on the inside but his exterior was humble as peace itself, he was waiting on the word from Nicky and when the call came he was beyond ready.

Joey wanted to hear the job through and through to make sure everything went according to plan, he wasn't in position to fuck up.

Andy was the last to come strolling into the bar, they were all there but came in separately. Louie was there and Joey kept all business outside of what Dutch already had going – Clear away from Louie, the two were light night and day.

Joey was just about to head to the basement when old man Pete came walking in with another made man of the family name Skinny Vinny, but only Vinny to anyone outside the family.

"Pete, Vinny, how you fellas feeling this morning,,"? Joey asked reaching out to give each man their proper respect.

Pete looked Joey up and down and give him a head nod.

"Did my fucking doctor tell you to ask me this shit,"? Vinny said more then asked as him and Pete brushed on by Joey as if he wasn't there.

Joey looked over at Louie, "I'll be downstairs if you need me,"

Nicky was standing over the pool table just looking at the $2 Million dollars, he had seen money and lots of it but there was nothing like thumb fucking through two million fucking dollars.

Bobby came out of the bathroom and looked everyone in the face, “where the fuck you guys come from,” He said with a laugh.

“Not that shit hole,” Tony shot back causing the whole room to laugh.

The men all shared small talk until the seen Joey hit the last set of steps.

Bobby, Nicky, Val, Andy, Willie, and Tony were all standing around the pool table neatly separating the piles of bills into small stacks.

"Who was the first man in the truck," Joey asked, taking a look around the table at each one of his men.

Nicky pointed to Tony.

"I was boss, we took –

"No need for any details , let's count this up and get the hell out of here before these old fucks come snooping," Joey chimed in cutting Tony off in mid sentence.

Tony took the lead and started counting the money, Joey was standing next to him helping as he separated the cut. Joey watched each mans reaction to the cut that Tony slide them, greed dug more graves then a shovel and Joey didn't want any holes around him.

The office use to be quite and clean, a place you could get some work done. But not today, there was more traffic then a whore house.

Jackson tapped the desk and got his partner attention, Allen looked up then around the room. He seen Jackson give him the head nod as telling him he was leaving out, he slowly stood and grabbed his gun from the desk and followed behind his partner.

“Let’s grab a bite and head over to the safe house,” Jackson said the moment Agent Allen came outside.

“Is this case still ours,”? Allen asked looking a little confused.

Jackson didn’t respond as he handed Allen a file, and opened the car door.

Allen didn’t open the file, he did exactly like his partner and got in the car and waited till they were away from the office.

“So what’s this about,”? Allen asked opening the thin stack of papers Jackson had given him.

“Well the vics mother made a statement after we placed her at the safe house, DelMarco wants us to get a full interrogation report then check back in with him,” Jackson informed his partner to the little that he knew himself.

Allen didn’t say a word as he sat back, this case was getting a little heavy a little to fast he was just praying it was a long day.

Dotty Winchester sat quietly at the wooden table, her full cup of black coffee untouched. Her mind was all over the place, her son was dead. She felt as if she were stuck in a horrible dream, a nightmare that scared her of, she wanted to wake up so bad but her reality was already there – Richie was gone.

Ms. Winchester was deeply in the thoughts of her mind, when Agent Jackson and Allen walked into the house. The two agents got all the way to the kitchen where Dotty sat before she know they were there, the tap on the counter got her attention.

"Oh my goodness, I thought I was alone,"? Dotty screamed, holding her hands palm flat against her chest.

"We didn't mean to frighten you Ms. Winchester were here about the statement you made to special agent DelMarco," Jackson said, waving a hard from himself to Allen as a show of them being alone

Ms. Winchester sat there for a Brief moment, the look in her eyes said many things but hurt and pain was the foundation.

## THE LULLABY

Louie sat there staring aimlessly out the bar's window, when a image came into his view. He looked back towards the two booths in the back and gave Old man Pete a nod with his head before grabbing his drink off the table and standing to his feet.

Joey's demeanor was nonchalant as he walked in the bar, fear was one thing – but power was another.

Pete got up and flipped the sign on the front door, just as Louie reached the bars counter top.

"You wanna tell me something," Louie said, standing over the bars sink washing his class.

Joey looked around, he stopped his eyes on Pete then slowly moved them over to Louie. "Yeah, Like what,"? Joey asked in return.

Louie took in a deep breath, the moment the air in his lungs released so it the bullshit. Joey didn't see it coming, but he sure felt when it got there.

Vinny gave the swing all he had,  the second the small bat hit Joey across the back it went flying through the room. The bat made a loud snap when it broke across Joey's back, the impact was lighter then it looked but Joey felt it as he went down on one knee.

Louie stood there next to old man Pete, the two looked on as Vinny and El'mo struggled to stand and hold Joey on his feet.

Joey calmly took in a deep breath, "you that dumb, trying this in my city,"? Joey asked, looking around at each man in the room.

"This city don't belong to no one," Louie snapped back.

"That's your fucking problem now, look around," -  old man Pete chimed in standing shoulder to shoulder with Louie. "Things turn sour when mothafuckas are to concerned with power."

Joey looked each man in the eyes as he glanced around the basement, he knew this wasn't a trap to death so his nerves were relaxed.

Louie never wore his necklace outside his shirt when he was up to something, Joey remembered hearing a old story as a kid about Louie never wanting his mother to witness his madness so he tucked in the small pendant that held her ashes.

Nicky stood by the back door waiting on a knock from Joey, he had called at 3 in the morning asking about a boat and to wait up for him – it was now 5 and the sun was know where in sight and neither was Joey.

They was a light tap at the back door, Nicky stood still and waited for the second knock. It was definitely Joey, he quickly turned the lock and slide the sliding door open.

Joey was dressed in all black from head to toe, one hand holding onto his book bag strap and the other on a small flip phone to his era. Nicky knew Joey his whole life, something was definitely different and his stomach started to bubble like the first day in school.

What the hell was going on, Nicky thought to himself as he stood there waiting to hear what Joey had to say.

Jackson stood over Allen's shoulder as he took down a address, Allen said thank you and hung up the phone.

"Looks like we're headed to Pike Creek, ever been,"? Allen asked as he looked back at Jackson.

"Price of living is to rich for my blood, is this the manager,"? Jackson replied asking.

"Yea, she's a 31 year old black female, Kris Green originally from Newark, New Jersey, been with the bank for about ten years, only one thing looks worthy of checking out,"

"And what's that,"? Jackson asked, taking a seat across from Allen's desk.

Allen moved the computer screen so his partner could get a better view of the monitor.

"What am I looking at,"?

Allen tapped his finger on the screen, they was a side note to the employment file.
It was a certificate for marriage license, it said she was married to a very familiar name to the two detectives.

Jackson stood up and rubbed a hand over his face, "you think this could actually be,"?

Allen looked around the station room, "let's have a dig," he replied with a devilish smile spreading across his face.

The two detectives didn't say another word as they grabbed a few things from the two desk and headed towards the car pool exit, they were headed to see this bank manager about her husband – or the husband about the wife.

El'mo stood along waiting for Marcy to step onto the elevator, the two had just flew in from Kentucky to Philadelphia international airport.

Her visit with Dutch went well, even after all these years he knew how to hold her together. Even when distance was ridiculous, Dutch made a way for her to come and go comfortably and she loved ever drop off him no matter his situation.

Marcy stepped onto the elevator with her bags, even with El'mo there at her aid she did everything on her own – she was from that era.

El'mo pressed five and waited for the doors to close, the two been away from home for a week now and you could that the two were ready to release and relax. Marcy was leaning her head up against the elevator walls as the small cart moved like lighten, El'mo was just as spaced out in thoughts of restlessness as she was.

Neither of the two were paying any attention to life, as they were both mentally resting on the elevator ride up to their car in the parking garage.

Mikey was calm as a human soul could be, the cold chill floating off of the concrete his back was tightly pressed against held him still. He took many risk, but a dumb move was never among them.

He heard the bell before he felt the elevator weight shift, palm calmly gripping ahold of the black metal in his hand.

El'mo stepped to the doors as they came open, holding his arm out for Marcy to exit the elevator. The nights air was a welcome from the mountains of Kentucky, Marcy hares every minute of the trips out there but she took them for her husband.

Mikey took one step and the space between the three was close like the next of kin, Marcy seen the flash but El'mo felt the bang.

El'mo never seen the bullet coming, soon as Marcy stepped off the elevator he was behind her – but so was Mikey.

The first shell hit El'mo head on, sending him crashing to the ground as he covered Marcy in blood along the way. Mikey spun the gun on Marcy the second he heard her lungs screamed for help.

I'm one motion Mikey had her off the ground and bound over his shoulders, her life was on a timer – and the clock holder was very impatient.

Marcy opened her eyes to total darkness, her clothes were soaking wet and she felt as cold as ice. She felt around but quickly noticed her hands were bound to what felt like handcuffs, her chest began to bounce rapidly as panic took over.

Mickey got the lights, the bright lights hanging overhead made it hard for Marcy to see as she held her hands up to her eyes. She was chained to the heating duck in a wet and flooded basement, her panic was beginning to creep into the max – her mind was all over the place.

“You take care of everything with the boat,”? Joey asked, taking a seat.

“Yeah, it’s all set – Nicky paused — you gonna tell me something or we doing this - Nicky pointed aimlessly around – whatever it is we’re even doing like it never happen,”? He asked, hoping Joey wasn’t keeping him in the dark.

Joey looked Nicky dead in the eyes, “would it really matter,”? He asked, not once breaking the look he held on his childhood friend.

“Whatever Secrets we have, their till death due us part,”

Joey shook his head in a yes manner, “So who’s car we taking,”?

Nicky watched Joey shoot a man in the face at the age of 13, it were times in life when you just knew things were real – and this – was one of those times and Nicky was starting to wonder if picking up the phone tonight was a bad idea.

DelMarco waited a few minutes past the meeting time before he picked up his phone to call out, Jackson picked up on the first ring.

"We're pulling in now," Jackson said putting the phone to his ear.

DelMarco didn't respond.

"Whatever these suits got planned I don't want to be involved, something is off about this whole ordeal," Allen cut in, as the two pulled in the underground parking garage.

Jackson looked over at his partner of 10 years, and the only thing he could do was nod his head.

DelMarco got to his feet and looked out the hotel window, he was about to introduce them to the major leagues – he just hoped he picked the right team.

Allen was the first to walk through the doors, he followed the rooms numbers once they got off the elevator. Jackson wasn't in a rush, or he just wasn't up for the shit either.

First familiar face Jackson seen was the mayor, he was the only one wearing a suit. This was definitely a different crowd, and Jackson was getting that same guy feeling from before.

A few minutes after the door shut, the vibes changed.

The mayor greeted both men immediately, his grip was firm and his stares were solid. Jackson took a seat and Allen stood, DelMarco was right beside the mayor and his men.

"Fellas, before we start let me explain that this meeting is a off the record occurrence to the public, this is to welcome a new task force to the safe of Delaware," The mayor paused and looked around the room, every face wore a confused look.

Jackson looked from the mayor then around the whole room before he raised his right hand.

Louie was cleaning up the bar when he seen the front doors push open, it was old man Pete and right behind him was Vinny. The two were having small talk and Louie went back to minding his business, he was waiting on a old friend himself.

Before Louie could get around the bar where Pete and vinny were and body came pushing through the front door, it was Louie's old time friend.

“Benny the fucking butcher, got damn friend,” Louie spoke the second Benny came into view.
Benny just laughed and closed the space between him and his old friend.

“Long time Lue,” Benny said, stepping back the the embrace the two held for a quick second.

Benny took a step back and looked around, he stopped on Old man Pete and Vinny. It was something about Pete that made him that he always adores once they were you guys, Pete was definitely one of the legendary gangstas from their era.

“Mr.Pete, how you been old timer,”? Benny asked taking a step away from Louie , he know Pete for many years but gangstas never liked reunions.

“How’s your father Benny,” Pete replied, handing his glass off to Vinny.

“All is well, thanks for asking,”

Pete looked Benny over from head to toe, “tell him pistol sends his love,” old man Pete replied.

Luke wasn't much of a drinker, but staring at bar lights and signs all night he started to think things over.

The Night was calming, and the wind felt good swimming through the open windows. Luke sat parked watching and waiting, the nights stars were the only beautiful within the sky.

A tall figure came walking from along the bar's side street, Luke watched as he pushed his way inside. Luke never seen the man before, so he waited.

30 minutes had passed Before Luke started the car, if they were witnesses inside by the time he went in - then it was out of his control. They just became Collateral damage!.

Louie and Benny had left out the back, and the second vinny heard the back door lock he jumped behind the bar.

“What you drinking old timer,”? Vinny asked in laughter, grabbing at glasses with one hand and a bottle of liquor with the other.

Old man Pete shook his head and cracked a smile, “Jack on the rocks,”

“Why does everyone call you old man Pete, your only what – Vinny paused – 50, nothing higher then 55,”?

“Only few know me as old man, Pete is my name – he paused – old man is my father, his name is Pete, Pistol Pete. People that know my old man call me old man out of respect for him, they say we sling pistols the same and people love that gangsta shit,”

Vinny didn’t know what to say to carry the conversation, he was 20 years younger then him. He tapped the bar and slide Pete his drink, “Tell me what you think old man,”

Old man Pete just looked grabbed the glass with a smile growing across his lips.

Neither of them were able to speak another word, as their attention was robbed the minute the front doors came swinging open. Pete quickly thought was a robbery no way someone would come for them, but the moment was faster then his thoughts.

Pete watched as the flame spit from the gun, it was like the world was standing still. He seen as the slug dig into Vinny's face, blood splashed the bar as he crashed into the bottles hitting the floor.

Old man Pete jumped to his feet, but Luke was young, tall and healthy he was within reach before Pete could even consider weather to fight or take flight.

The first shell smashed into his mouth, his neck snapped so hard Luke thought he shot twice. Pete fell to the hardwood floor like a sack of potatoes, by the time Luke stepped over his body there was a pool of blood surrounding his head.

Luke looked down and shook his head, "guess you can tell your mother that you didn't have a hard head after all," Luke said to himself as he spun around to leave.

Jackson was ready by five o'clock the next morning, he was the first agent in the office waiting for his emergency meeting.

Allen came in right behind a few other agents assigned to the case, but Jackson didn't want to see anyone but the mayor. He wanted to know just who they were after, because it was starting to keep him up at night.

The mayor came in along side of DelMarco, the two were engaged in deep conversation. Jackson had a feeling

DelMarco was keeping everyone else out the loop, but for what reasons exactly- he kept asking himself.

The mayor walked over to where Jackson stood, “Hey Kevin, let me speak to you for a moment,”

Jackson nodded and stepped to the side.

“I read your email, it’s definitely appropriate to say someone is fucking someone over,”? The mayor asked.

“Well from what the bank’s manager had to say, down to our vics mother and the link back. It’s definitely appropriate, but who’s crew is this coming from,”? Jackson replied asking is own question.

The mayor said a few more things to Jackson before calling the attention of everyone in the room, “DelMarco hit the lights, is they screen set up and ready,”? He asked, pulling out a small remote from his blazer pocket.

DelMarco didn’t reply and the screen came up on the wall, everything was good.

“The victims mother said the son liked to gamble, often hung out in Organized crime owned establishments, so this maybe a inside job. One thing we know for sure is that the two cases are related, The interview with the bank manager revealed that Richie did however confined in someone that he owed a lot of money for a gambling debt but she expressed that he did not wear a worried or concerned look as if it was a large amount, definitely nothing worth killing over. But she stated that was months ago on a company trip to the Cayman Islands, the two often spoke outside of work.”

“Anything sexual between the two,”? Allen asked.

“No, the bank manager is married, husband is actually doing federal time on drug trafficking charges in Philadelphia, nothing in relation or even connected.” DelMarco chimed in, pointing to pictures as he spoke.

Joey was waiting for his brother at the boat yard, it was almost 15 minutes past the meeting time and he was beginning to worry. No call from either side, he was started to think things back fired.

Nicky came out the back room, “Any word yet,”? He asked looking out the window of the boat.

“Nah, nothing, not a sound,” Joey replied

“Don’t speak your soon, I got four headlights coming down,” Nicky whispered waving back for Joey to get up and look.

Four sets of lights came creeping down the dirt road towards the boating docks, Joey recognized the car’s automatically.

Bobby got low along the same window, “We moving on sight,”? He asked, taking up a place next to them.

“No, my brother got other plans for them,” Joey replied looking over to the two boats facing them. Joey pulled out a phone from his pocket and checked the screen, everything was going smooth.

Val pulled in and parked, the second car pulled in and killed the lights. Joey seen Val and came up from the boats deck, Mikey was the first one too see them.

“Got a bag in the trunk,” Mikey said, tapping the back of the black Cadillac.

Joey gave Mikey a head nod, Val came around the back of the trunk we’re the two stood.

“Holy shit, what the fuck,” Val barked out, swinging his head from Joey to Mikey trying to understand.

Mikey put a gun to his forehead the second he turned back to look at him, “how long did you knew Val,” Joey asked, stepping around to look Val in the eyes.

“What the fuck are you talking about,”? Valentino asked, looking more confused then a child lost in the Big Apple.

“Richie,” Joey asked.

Val looked even more confused, he never met Richie until Joey came to them with the plans to hit the truck. "You brung him around,"

Mikey pushes the gun deeper into his face, "The name Chuck Winchester sound familiar,"? Joey asked, looking Val dead in the face only a few inches from him.

Val looked Joey in the face, "What about him Joey, we were kids that's not our era," Val replied shaking his head from left to right.

Joey looked over at Mikey, "let's take this party inside,"

Luke was standing there when Joey walked everybody on board, the party was in full swing now Luke thought to himself.

Marcy was the first one on followed by Mikey, Joey and Bobby walked Val on as Nicky closed the door behind them.

It seemed like everyone knew what was going – at least Marcy thought so. She sat there confused and scared beyond her worst.

Luke waited until everyone was seated, he slide the glass door open and joined the party out on the floor deck, it was just at waters height.

Luke placed a small phone on the table and took a step back, a strong voice came over the tiny cell phone.

“Long time Marcy, hows that old fuck doing,”? Jesse asked, letting a light chuckle go into the phone. The room was quite, but right now the only sound was the Ocean. Even at close look it seemed like everyone on the deck stopped breathing,

Marcy didn’t say a word, neither did anyone else for that matter.

“Marcy do you want to tell the rest of the family why we’re all here tonight, or do you want me too,”? Jesse asked, as every eye in the room was on the small phone like the man was standing there in the flesh.

“I hope you rot in that fucking bucket,” Marcy screamed,

Jesse was laughing so hard on the other end of the phone you could actually see it moving, his laugh sent chills through the room. If there was a recording of the devils laugh, it was his by a long shot.

“I guess we can have a open Discussion since the cat got everyone’s tongue,” Jesse replied you anyone listening.

Joey leaned against the boats railing and listened to his brother,, the breeze was definitely feeling good tonight.

"In 1988 there was a Federal organize crime trial going on in New York, come to find out they had a star witness here in Delaware. Once the feds got to asking more about the witness to the agent over seeing the informant, soon they wanted to know more about Delaware. In 1989 the feds finally got a netting with this informant, court records are sealed but the original transcripts state everything. Jesse paused for a quick second,

"Louie was never away on business when the feds got Dutch, he was in New York – he never missed the indictment- he was the fucking indictment, Jesse stopped. "Marcy at any time don't feel scared to jump in," he laughed.

"Dutch let Louie bury every single one of them, and for what – so they would take away the death penalty, he stood aside and let that rat bitch destroy the whole family. Louie kept things going for Dutch, he left out many of his houses and establishments and to many that alone is suspect but what the fuck is more suspect then harboring a fucking rat for almost 20 years,"

The boat was still and the only sounds we're the water, a car off in the distance every now and again.

"I took my time like a man, I was only 23 then the feds got me, I was young and still had so much ahead of myself, yeah yeah yeah – I heard all that shit but I picked my path and I walked it like a fucking man. But my that's not why we're here, right,"? Jesse asked, but no one gave a reply.

“Chuck Winchester sound familiar Marcy,”? Jesse asked, listening to the other end, from his end it sounded like a abandoned call.

“No I don’t know that name,” Marcy cried, holding her chest tight.

Jesse didn’t say a word, “what about you Val,”? He asked Valentino

Val looked around the boat, he know these dudes since he could remember, all this wasn’t making any sense to him. He heard stories but nothing that concerned him or any of them – at least that’s how he felt.

Luke moved around to the opposite, everyone on the boat was now in front of him. He looked down and around to each one, he was waiting to he his brothers voice.

Jesse made a few sounds in the back, he sounded as though he was walking up stairs because his breathing became stronger.

“Remember the day your old man died,”? Jesse asked a question, no one other then Val spoke up.

“Yeah, You, Luke and Joey came to my mothers house, it was the only thing keeping me together,” Val replied looking at the phone as if Jesse was seating on the table instead of the phone.

“Well the day your father died was the day Chuck realized that the rat that put him away was still living and well, Louie was named your fathers brother and best man since birth, the name lullaby stayed at the forefront of his mind each day he awoke inside these grimey penitentiary walls. Dutch made that cover possible for all these years, and Marcy your telling us that this is all new to you,”? Jesse asked.

“That’s one lier,” Jesse said, and the second those words left his mouth so did a 40 Caliber shell from Luke’s gun went ripping from the back to a grand opening of Marcy’s face. Blood splashed like a balloon popping from a rooftop drop, she was definitely dead on impact.

Every face on the boat covered in panic, death was common to some but in person was rare. Jesse laughed like a kid in a candy store, something he waited so long to see was now here.

“I wasn’t raised by my father, my mother took care of us. She once told me – greed digs more graves then a shovel, and to this day this saying is tattooed on my left arm,” Jesse paused for a brief moment, “And Val, you not kept your mouth shut for the money they slide you for knowing the secrets, your just as bad as the rat that told,”

Val’s head popped louder then the gun itself, he fell towards the deck but Joey sent a fast kick sending him falling for the water. No one moved to save him, and no one said a word.

Freddy pulled out a bandana and swiped the sweat from his forehead, he heat  pumping from the cooker was reaching a new temperature – or Freddy thoughts so.

"Freddy your nephews are here," Karl yelled from the front, he stood there watching as his nephews came strolling into the Funeral home.

"Uncle Karl, how you doing,? Joey asked, reaching out to hug his uncle.

The three stood around talking until Freddy came from the back doors, he was sweating like he just came back from a 5 mile run.

"Nephews," Freddy yelled throwing up his thick arms, Joey stepped up first and Luke.
"Let's take this to the back,"

Karl told them he had to take care of a few things and said his goodbyes and see you another time before he disappeared and the three were left alone.

Luke pulled the same small phone from his pocket, after a few clicks he placed it to his ear.

Freddy smiles from ear to ear when he heard his nephew voice come beaming over the opposite end, and the love was shared because Jesse's voiced never sounded more alive.

"Talk to me unc, tell me something good," Jesse spike into the phone.

"Tell Chuck to look towards the second gun tower," Freddy replied into the phone, he could hear another voice in the background but to far to hear what was said.

"All eyes unc," Jesse replied back.

“Now look to the sky, thought I would said his rat ass to you in a hand ball, it was chuck’s favorite game as a kid,” he replied, Freddy didn’t wait for a reply, he know what was already understood never had to be explained.

Luke looked over to his uncle with a curious face, “so what you do unc,”? Luke asked, breaking his look to glance over at his brother.

Joey looked at both men, one to the other and just waited until they decided on who would speak first.

Freddy seen the wonder, “I sent them Louie’s head, I cremated His whole fucking head, I thought Chuck would like to piss in his face one time before it’s all said and done,”

Joey looked more happy then surprised, he seen some shit in his life but nothing this fucking gangsta, he smiled and shook his head.

Luke didn’t show one sign, he was hard to read and was mostly humble every second but tonight he seemed more relaxed.

“I wanted a long time to hear that type of joy in my brothers voice, it’s amazing what one could find peace in,” Luke said and smiled.

Luke looked down at his uncles hand, he was trying to pass him the small phone.

“Make sure Chuck’s wife is taken care of, and pay for his son funeral expenses, his father thinks  it’s best to move on like today never happen, so it will come as a shock to hear the news of his son murder,”

Joey and Luke both reached out and embraced Their uncle.

Luke stopped in his tracks, “hey unc, so Richie was chucks son,”?

Freddy looked back at his nephews,” sometimes you gotta make a sacrifice for what you believe in,”

Jesse closed the flip phone and slide it back in his pocket, he watched as Chuck picked the hard ball up and rolled it around in one hand before he walked away.

The yard lights clicked on and the man inside  tower came yelling over the intercom, “one hour till recall,”

Jesse got to his feet and began spinning the jails compound, Dutch was a dead man and he knew it. He just wished to be there the moment death knocks on his cell door, but no matter what Jesse took the don from the table and it was all his. His father would be proud of him, but in some ways Jesse thought different.

One bad apple could never really spoil the bunch, the roots are a trees foundation in strength - it's never about what drops from the top, only what grows after.

Secrets, Till death due is part.



*ACKNOWLEDGEMENTS*

I would like to Take the moment to give all praise to Allah, through you all things are possible. May you continue to bless my Journey and clear unwanted attention from my path. Allah is Great.

To my young kings, Aaron Jr, Asir, Amir, I love you guys to death and I'm very grateful to have you kids and I thank Allah daily for the amazing job your mothers do,(Christina & Shantel). Kris we will always be connected by heart, I love you and miss you.

My brother, Jason Shaw (in the book as Luke) lol man I love you bro, nothing or no one could ever break the bond we hold. We came from nothing #CFN #PRESSFIVE
WE ALL WE GOT AND NEED (you know the vibes )
#TINAKIDS

My sisters I love y'all, #MOMMASBABIES #CFN

My uncle Freddy ( As in the book) Alfred Shaw, your always in my corner and for that I am blessed. You tell me just about every time we speak that grandma and mommy would be proud of me and I truly believe that myself. I love you unc, thanks for all the love you give. #FAMILY

Angel Colbert, I'm so proud of you baby girl please chase every dream you ever have I'm forever rooting for you. #FAMILY

Justice Shaw (I know your married lol) I love you and I'm so proud of you you know we speak all the time. Your so smart and ambitious I hope you go so far in this life and leave a legacy for others. #FAMILY

Jermaine Colbert (Diddy) I love you boi, I know your young and it feels like you got the world on your shoulders but trust me – it gets greater later. I love you baby boi I'm proud of the young man your becoming. #FAMILY

Family Is Everything.

To my loving mother, I miss you more each day, the saying it heals with time - that's a fucking lie (and excuse my language) but it only gets worse. I wish you we're here to enjoy these moments and see my sons grow, but it's only temporary we will all be together again one day, till then hold us a spot. We love and miss you #TINAMORRIS
#QUEENB #FUCKCANCER (Me & Jason just celebrated our birthdays, wish you could of smoked one with us) FOREVER TINAS BABIES

IN LOVING MEMORY OF JUNNIE
This Toast Is For You

First & Foremost, Put ya Rollie's to the sky, we miss y'all down here. This for all the fallen soldiers, weather killed by friends or foes.

To My whole team, P.F BOYZ we ain't going no where so PRESS FIVE and listen to the voice of the streets. #CFN #PRESSFIVE #MDH 4LI7E we all we got and need!

FREE THE JAILS, STATE, FEDERAL , COUNTY, CENTER, whatever you in keep ya head up, the fight is never over. Fuck those who stand to oppose!!!!!

Ninja, miss you bro, fuck the feds this fight ain't over. Hold ya head up blood it's forever free you till they free you. (Church) Brooklyn's most hated #PRESSFIVE #EGB #MDH

If da god,) miss you too bro, still mad you ain't listen to me. It's free you till they free you shine, BX stand up. Boston Rd.

Seven, can't wait till you touch down. We gonna make history, them mafuckas thought we made the jails shake wait till they feel the ground bounce lol love you boi see you soon North Carolina stand up. Kilo, Trill, Sosa, Streets, Noonie, Mattie Rich, the whole team 7 yktv twin, LMB'zup

So many people to name and remember, like I always say - if I miss you it's nothing personal. I been all over the world it's hard to remember at times but that don't mean I forgot you in life, I got love for everybody that got love for me.

All my bro's behind them walls, I love y'all. I Press Five for y'all FREE THE JAILS

To all my bro's in these streets, I love y'all. Stay dangerous Delaware, New York, Connecticut, Maryland, New Jersey, Pennsylvania, Virginia, North Carolina, Atlanta, South Carolina, Tennessee, California, Texas, Louisiana, Portland Oregon, the whole map and back.

SECRETS (2020) PRESS FIVE PUBLISHING ™

TRUST IS RARE: AMAZON.COM
AARON MORRIS
PUBLISHED: JANUARY 17th 2020 (ebooks available)

More updates and events follow us on social media:

@offcicalpressfive
@pressfive_books
FB: Aaron Smooth Morris
For more information please contact: PRESS FIVE PUBLISHING.
Email: pressfivebooks@gmail.com

Made in the USA
Middletown, DE
13 March 2022